JP
ROD

Rodgers, Frank, 1944-
Doodle dog.

$12.95

DATE			

Doodle Dog

Copyright © 1990 by Frank Rodgers
All rights reserved.
CIP data is available.
First published in the United States in 1990 by
Dutton Children's Books,
a division of Penguin Books USA Inc.
Published simultaneously in Canada by
Fitzhenry & Whiteside Limited, Toronto
Originally published in Great Britain in 1990 by
William Heinemann Ltd., Michelin House
81 Fulham Road, London SW3 6RB
ISBN 0-525-44585-4
Produced by Mandarin
Printed and bound in Hong Kong
First Edition   10 9 8 7 6 5 4 3 2 1

Doodle Dog

Frank Rodgers

DUTTON CHILDREN'S BOOKS · NEW YORK

Sam was playing with his toys on the
kitchen table while his mother was chopping
carrots.

"Mom," he said suddenly, "could I have a dog? Please?" he added, before his mother had to remind him.

"I'm sorry, Sam," she said. "An apartment is no place to keep a dog. It wouldn't be fair to the dog."

"What about a very small dog? A really tiny one?" Sam asked hopefully.

"Not even a puppy that could sit in a teacup, like your toy bear," said his mother. "Even little dogs need space."

Sam didn't like the idea of a dog in a teacup anyway.

Sam opened one of his books and pointed to a picture. "That's the kind of dog I want," he said.

His mother looked at the picture of a little puppy in a barnyard. "He *is* nice," she said.

"If he were my dog, I would teach him to do tricks," said Sam. "He would shake hands,

fetch a stick,

balance a biscuit on his nose, and catch a ball in midair.

And he could sleep the foot of my bed."

"Maybe we'll get a dog if we move someday," Sam's mother said. "But for now, why don't you get your crayons and draw one?"

So he did.

"See my dog, Mom?" said Sam a few minutes later.

"It's terrific!" said his mother.

Sam frowned. It's okay, I guess," he said, "but could you help me draw a better one?"

His mother laughed. "I'm not very good at drawing, but I'll try," she said. She helped Sam sketch the outline of a dog on his paper. "I'm afraid this is really just a doodle," she said.

"Doodle," said Sam. "That's a good name for a dog. I'm going to call him Doodle."

"Why don't you color him in?" his mother suggested.

"All right," said Sam. He gave Doodle
black ears, a black tail, some brown patches,
and spots on his tummy.
   "He looks so friendly!" exclaimed his
mother.
   "He looks like a real dog," said Sam.

Sam liked the picture so much that he put it
on his bed before he went to sleep that night.
"Good night, Doodle," he whispered.

The next morning, Sam felt something tickle
his cheek. He opened his eyes and stared.
Doodle was licking his face!

"Is it really you, Doodle?" he laughed.

"Woof!" barked Doodle, and Sam knew that
he meant, "Of course!"

Sam gave Doodle an enormous hug. Doodle
wagged his tail.

Sam jumped out of bed and got dressed.
"Can you do tricks, Doodle?" he asked.

Doodle jumped off the bed and stood on his
hind legs. Then he looked up at Sam as if to
say, "What do you think of that?"

Sam laughed. "You're just the kind of dog I've always wanted. What else can you do?"

Sam picked up a ball and put it on Doodle's nose.

First Doodle balanced the ball. Then he tossed it way up to the ceiling. When it came back down, he jumped and caught it in his mouth.

"Hurray!" shouted Sam. "You're the best dog in the world. Shake hands?" Doodle lifted his paw for Sam to shake.

"Boy, you're smart. You'd be a good sheepdog," said Sam. "Come and see my farm."

Sam took out his toy farm set.

He made a square fence and put the little wooden animals inside. "This is our farm, Doodle," he said. "Let's go in."

And suddenly, there they stood, in the middle of the barnyard. Sam and Doodle heard the sounds of farm animals all around them. Hens clucked and cows mooed. Ducks quacked and pigs grunted.

The sheep were the noisiest of all. They were bleating loudly and running all over the farm.

"Quick, Doodle," said Sam. "Let's round up the sheep."

"Yip!" barked Doodle, which meant, "Sure!"

Doodle was a wonderful sheepdog. He dashed here and there,

snuck up behind the sheep,

and helped Sam herd them back into the pasture.

Sam closed the gate. "We did it!" he said.
"Good job, Doodle!"

Doodle wagged his tail and barked, "Ruff,
yip, yip, ruff!" which meant, "Now let's
explore the farm!"

Sam and Doodle saw
the hens and their chicks,

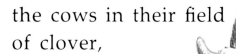

the ducks on the pond,

the cows in their field
of clover,

the pigs in their sty,

and the goat in its pen.

They smelled the warm summer smells of the country, and Sam threw sticks for Doodle to fetch. Then they went into the big barn.

The air inside was warm and still, and
sunlight flickered through cracks in the walls.
The loft was filled with big bales of hay.

Loose hay was scattered around the bottom of the ladder. "Let's get to work, Doodle," said Sam.

He lifted a big armful of hay, and Doodle pushed some into a pile with his nose.

Soon the barn looked neat and clean. "Grr, woof, yip," barked Doodle. Sam knew he meant, "What next?" And from the other side of the barn, someone answered, "Neighhhh!"

Sam and Doodle looked around. In the corner was a stall, and standing in the stall was a beautiful pony. It neighed again as if to say, ''Come and talk to me!''

"You were so quiet we didn't notice you,"
said Sam as he stroked the pony's nose. The
pony nodded its head and gently took the hay
he offered.

"Time for breakfast, Sam," called his mother.

"Coming, Mom," Sam answered. "Ready to go, Doodle?"

Doodle didn't answer.
He was gone. Sam
looked down and saw
his picture on the floor.

"I'll carry you, Doodle," he said, picking up
the paper.

As Sam walked toward the kitchen, he
looked at the drawing and smiled. "That was
fun, Doodle," he said. "Let's go to the park
after breakfast."